Dante
and the
Lobster

D0785872

**Faber
Stories**

Samuel Beckett was born in Dublin in 1906 and graduated from Trinity College. He settled in Paris in 1937, after travels in Germany and periods of residence in London and Dublin. He remained in France during the Second World War and was active in the French Resistance. From the spring of 1946 his plays, novels, short fiction, poetry and criticism were largely written in French. With the production of *En attendant Godot* in Paris in 1953, Beckett's work began to achieve widespread recognition. During his subsequent career as a playwright and novelist in both French and English he redefined the possibilities of prose fiction and writing for the theatre. Samuel Beckett won the Prix Formentor in 1961 and the Nobel Prize in Literature in 1969. He died in Paris in December 1989.

Samuel Beckett

Dante and the Lobster

Faber Stories

ff

First published in this single edition in 2019
by Faber & Faber Limited
Bloomsbury House
74–77 Great Russell Street
London WC1B 3DA

Originally published by Chatto & Windus in 1934
First published by Faber in *More Pricks Than Kicks* in 2010

Typeset by Faber & Faber Limited
Printed and bound by CPI Group (UK) Ltd, Croydon, CR0 4YY

A CIP record for this book
is available from the British Library

ISBN 978–0–571–35180–0

MIX
Paper from
responsible sources
FSC® C020471

10 9 8 7 6 5 4 3 2 1

It was morning and Belacqua was stuck in the first of the canti in the moon. He was so bogged that he could move neither backward nor forward. Blissful Beatrice was there, Dante also, and she explained the spots on the moon to him. She shewed him in the first place where he was at fault, then she put up her own explanation. She had it from God, therefore he could rely on its being accurate in every particular. All he had to do was to follow her step by step. Part one, the refutation, was plain sailing. She made her point clearly, she said what she had to say without fuss or loss of time. But part two, the demonstration, was so dense that Belacqua could not make head or tail of it. The disproof, the reproof, that was patent. But then came the proof, a rapid shorthand of the real facts, and Belacqua was bogged indeed. Bored also, impatient to get on to Piccarda. Still he pored over the enigma, he would not concede himself conquered, he would understand at least the meanings of the words, the order in which they were spoken and the nature of the satisfaction that they conferred on the misinformed poet, so that when they were ended he was refreshed and could raise his heavy head, intending to return thanks and make formal retraction of his old opinion.

He was still running his brain against this impenetrable passage when he heard midday strike. At once he switched his mind off its task. He scooped his fingers under the book and shovelled it back till it lay wholly on his palms. The Divine Comedy face upward on the lectern of his palms. Thus disposed he raised it under his nose and there he slammed it shut. He held it aloft for a time, squinting at it angrily, pressing the boards inwards with the heels of his hands. Then he laid it aside.

He leaned back in his chair to feel his mind subside and the itch of this mean quodlibet die down. Nothing could be done until his mind got better and was still, which gradually it did. Then he ventured to consider what he had to do next. There was always something that one had to do next. Three large obligations presented themselves. First lunch, then the lobster, then the Italian lesson. That would do to be going on with. After the Italian lesson he had no very clear idea. No doubt some niggling curriculum had been drawn up by someone for the late afternoon and evening, but he did not know what. In any case it did not matter. What did matter was: one, lunch; two, the lobster; three, the

Italian lesson. That was more than enough to be going on with.

Lunch, to come off at all, was a very nice affair. If his lunch was to be enjoyable, and it could be very enjoyable indeed, he must be left in absolute tranquillity to prepare it. But if he were disturbed now, if some brisk tattler were to come bouncing in now big with a big idea or a petition, he might just as well not eat at all, for the food would turn to bitterness on his palate, or, worse again, taste of nothing. He must be left strictly alone, he must have complete quiet and privacy, to prepare the food for his lunch.

The first thing to do was to lock the door. Now nobody could come at him. He deployed an old *Herald* and smoothed it out on the table. The rather handsome face of McCabe the assassin stared up at him. Then he lit the gas-ring and unhooked the square flat toaster, asbestos grill, from its nail and set it precisely on the flame. He found he had to lower the flame. Toast must not on any account be done too rapidly. For bread to be toasted as it ought, through and through, it must be done on a mild steady flame. Otherwise you only charred the outsides and left the pith as sodden as before. If there was one thing he abominated more than another it was to feel his teeth meet in a bathos of pith and dough. And it was so easy to do the thing properly. So, he thought, having regulated the flow and adjusted the grill, by the time I have the bread cut that will be just right. Now the long barrel-loaf came out of its biscuit-tin and had its end evened off on the face of McCabe. Two inexorable drives with the bread-saw and a pair of neat rounds of raw bread, the main elements of his meal, lay before him, awaiting his pleasure. The stump of the loaf went back into prison, the crumbs, as though there were no such thing as a sparrow in the wide world, were swept in a fever away, and the slices snatched up and carried to the grill. All these preliminaries were very hasty and impersonal.

It was now that real skill began to be required, it was at this point that the average person began to make a hash of the entire proceedings. He laid his cheek against the soft of the bread, it was spongy and warm, alive. But he would very soon take that plush feel off it, by God but he would very quickly take that fat white look off its face. He lowered the gas a suspicion and plaqued one flabby slab plump down on the glowing fabric, but very pat and precise, so that the whole resembled the Japanese flag. Then on top, there not being room for the two to do evenly side by side, and if you did not do them evenly you might just as well save yourself the trouble of doing them at all, the other round was set to warm. When the first candidate was done, which was only when it was black through and through, it changed places with its comrade, so that now it in its turn lay on top, done to a dead end, black and smoking, waiting till as much could be said of the other.

For the tiller of the field the thing was simple, he had it from his mother. The spots were Cain with his truss of thorns, dispossessed, cursed from the earth, fugitive and vagabond. The moon was that countenance fallen and branded, seared with the first stigma of God's pity, that an outcast might not die quickly. It was a mix-up in the mind of the tiller, but that did not matter. It had been good enough for his mother, it was good enough for him.

Belacqua on his knees before the flame, poring over the grill, controlled every phase of the broiling. It took time, but if a thing was worth doing at all it was worth doing well, that was a true saying. Long before the end the room was full of smoke and the reek of burning. He switched off the gas, when all that human care and skill could do had been done, and restored the toaster to its nail. This was an act of dilapidation, for it seared a great weal in the paper. This was hooliganism pure and simple. What the hell did he care? Was it his wall? The same hopeless paper had been there fifty years. It was livid with age. It could not be disimproved.

Next a thick paste of Savora, salt and Cayenne on each round, well worked in while the pores were still open with the heat. No butter, God forbid, just a good foment of mustard and salt and pepper on each round. Butter was a blunder, it made the toast soggy. Buttered toast was all right for Senior Fellows and Salvationists, for such as had nothing but false teeth in their heads. It was no good at all to a fairly strong young rose like Belacqua. This meal that he was at such pains to make ready, he would devour it with a sense of rapture and victory, it would be like smiting the sledded Polacks on the ice. He would snap at it with closed eyes, he would gnash it into a pulp, he would vanquish it utterly with his fangs. Then the anguish of pungency, the pang of the spices, as each mouthful died, scorching his palate, bringing tears.

But he was not yet all set, there was yet much to be done. He had burnt his offering, he had not fully dressed it. Yes, he had put the horse behind the tumbrel.

He clapped the toasted rounds together, he brought them smartly together like cymbals, they clave the one to the other on the viscid salve of Savora. Then he wrapped them up for the time being in any old sheet of paper. Then he made himself ready for the road.

Now the great thing was to avoid being accosted. To be stopped at this stage and have conversational nuisance committed all over him would be a disaster. His whole being was straining forward towards the joy in store. If he were accosted now he might just as well fling his lunch into the gutter and walk straight back home. Sometimes his hunger, more of mind, I need scarcely say, than of body, for this meal amounted to such a frenzy that he would not have hesitated to strike any man rash enough to buttonhole and baulk him, he would have shouldered him out of his path without ceremony. Woe betide the meddler who crossed him when his mind was really set on this meal.

He threaded his way rapidly, his head bowed, through a familiar labyrinth of lanes and suddenly dived into a little family grocery. In the shop they were not surprised. Most days, about this hour, he shot in off the street in this way.

The slab of cheese was prepared. Separated since morning from the piece, it was only waiting for Belacqua to call and take it. Gorgonzola cheese. He knew a man who came from Gorgonzola, his name was Angelo. He had been born in Nice but all his youth had been spent in Gorgonzola. He knew where to look for it. Every day it was there, in the same corner, waiting to be called for. They were very decent obliging people.

He looked sceptically at the cut of cheese. He turned it over on its back to see was the other side any better. The other side was worse. They had laid it better side up, they had practised that little deception. Who shall blame them? He rubbed it. It was sweating. That was something. He stooped and smelt it. A faint fragrance of corruption. What good was that? He didn't want fragrance, he wasn't a bloody gourmet, he wanted a good stench. What he wanted was a good green stenching rotten lump of Gorgonzola cheese, alive, and by God he would have it.

He looked fiercely at the grocer.

'What's that?' he demanded.

The grocer writhed.

'Well?' demanded Belacqua, he was without fear when roused, 'is that the best you can do?'

'In the length and breadth of Dublin' said the grocer 'you won't find a rottener bit this minute.'

Belacqua was furious. The impudent dogsbody, for two pins he would assault him.

'It won't do' he cried, 'do you hear me, it won't do at all. I won't have it.' He ground his teeth.

The grocer, instead of simply washing his hands like Pilate, flung out his arms in a wild crucified gesture of supplication. Sullenly Belacqua undid his packet and slipped the cadaverous tablet of cheese between the hard cold black boards of the toast. He stumped to the door where he whirled round however.

'You heard me?' he cried.

'Sir' said the grocer. This was not a question, nor yet an expression of acquiescence. The tone in which it was let fall made it quite impossible to know what was in the man's mind. It was a most ingenious riposte.

'I tell you' said Belacqua with great heat 'this won't do at all. If you can't do better than this' he raised the hand that held the packet 'I shall be obliged to go for my cheese elsewhere. Do you mark me?'

'Sir' said the grocer.

He came to the threshold of his store and watched the indignant customer hobble away. Belacqua had a spavined gait, his feet were in ruins, he suffered with them almost continuously. Even in the night they took no rest, or next to none. For then the cramps took over from the corns and hammer-toes, and carried on. So that he would press the fringes of his

14

feet desperately against the end-rail of the bed or, better again, reach down with his hand and drag them up and back towards the instep. Skill and patience could disperse the pain, but there it was, complicating his night's rest.

The grocer, without closing his eyes or taking them off the receding figure, blew his nose in the skirt of his apron. Being a warm-hearted human man he felt sympathy and pity for this queer customer who always looked ill and dejected. But at the same time he was a small tradesman, don't forget that, with a small tradesman's sense of personal dignity and what was what. Thruppence, he cast it up, thruppence worth of cheese per day, one and a tanner per week. No, he would fawn on no man for that, no, not on the best in the land. He had his pride.

15

Stumbling along by devious ways towards the lowly public where he was expected, in the sense that the entry of his grotesque person would provoke no comment or laughter, Belacqua gradually got the upper hand of his choler. Now that lunch was as good as a *fait accompli,* because the incontinent bosthoons of his own class, itching to pass on a big idea or inflict an appointment, were seldom at large in this shabby quarter of the city, he was free to consider items two and three, the lobster and the lesson, in closer detail.

At a quarter to three he was due at the School. Say five to three. The public closed, the fishmonger reopened, at half-past two. Assuming then that his lousy old bitch of an aunt had given her order in good time that morning, with strict injunctions that it should be ready and waiting so that her blackguard boy should on no account be delayed when he called for it first thing in the afternoon, it would be time enough if he left the public as it closed, he could remain on till the last moment. Benissimo. He had half-a-crown. That was two pints of draught anyway and perhaps a bottle to wind up with. Their bottled stout was particularly excellent and well up. And he would still be left with enough coppers to buy a *Herald* and take a tram if he felt tired or was pinched for time. Always assuming, of course, that the lobster was all ready to be handed over. God damn these tradesmen, he thought, you can never rely on them. He had not done an exercise but that did not matter. His Professoressa was so charming and remarkable. Signorina Adriana Ottolenghi! He did not believe it possible for a woman to be more intelligent or better informed than the

17

little Ottolenghi. So he had set her on a pedestal in his mind, apart from other women. She had said last day that they would read *Il Cinque Maggio* together. But she would not mind if he told her, as he proposed to, in Italian, he would frame a shining phrase on his way from the public, that he would prefer to postpone the *Cinque Maggio* to another occasion. Manzoni was an old woman, Napoleon was another. *Napoleone di mezza calzetta, fa l'amore a Giacominetta.* Why did he think of Manzoni as an old woman? Why did he do him that injustice? Pellico was another. They were all old maids, suffragettes. He must ask his Signorina where he could have received that impression, that the 19th century in Italy was full of old hens trying to cluck like Pindar. Carducci was another. Also about the spots on the moon. If she could not tell him there and then she would make it up, only too gladly, against the next time. Everything was all set now and in order. Barring, of course, the lobster, which had to remain an incalculable factor. He must just hope for the best. And expect the worst, he thought gaily, diving into the public, as usual.

Belacqua drew near to the school, quite happy, for all had gone swimmingly. The lunch had been a notable success, it would abide as a standard in his mind. Indeed he could not imagine its ever being superseded. And such a pale soapy piece of cheese to prove so strong! He must only conclude that he had been abusing himself all these years in relating the strength of cheese directly to its greenness. We live and learn, that was a true saying. Also his teeth and jaws had been in heaven, splinters of vanquished toast spraying forth at each gnash. It was like eating glass. His mouth burned and ached with the exploit. Then the food had been further spiced by the intelligence, transmitted in a low tragic voice across the counter by Oliver the improver, that the Malahide murderer's petition for mercy, signed by half the land, having been rejected, the man must swing at dawn in Mountjoy and nothing could save him. Ellis the hangman was even now on his way. Belacqua, tearing at the sandwich and swilling the precious stout, pondered on McCabe in his cell.

The lobster was ready after all, the man handed it over instanter, and with such a pleasant smile. Really a little bit of courtesy and goodwill went a long way in this world.

A smile and a cheerful word from a common working-man and the face of the world was brightened. And it was so easy, a mere question of muscular control.

'Lepping' he said cheerfully, handing it over.

'Lepping?' said Belacqua. What on earth was that?

'Lepping fresh, sir' said the man, 'fresh in this morning.'

Now Belacqua, on the analogy of mackerel and other fish that he had heard described as lepping fresh when they had been taken but an hour or two previously, supposed the man to mean that the lobster had very recently been killed.

Signorina Adriana Ottolenghi was waiting in the little front room off the hall, which Belacqua was naturally inclined to think of rather as the vestibule. That was her room, the Italian room. On the same side, but at the back, was the French room. God knows where the German room was. Who cared about the German room anyway?

He hung up his coat and hat, laid the long knobby brown-paper parcel on the hall-table, and went prestly in to the Ottolenghi.

After about half-an-hour of this and that obiter, she complimented him on his grasp of the language.

'You make rapid progress' she said in her ruined voice.

There subsisted as much of the Ottolenghi as might be expected to of the person of a lady of a certain age who had found being young and beautiful and pure more of a bore than anything else.

Belacqua, dissembling his great pleasure, laid open the moon enigma.

'Yes' she said 'I know the passage. It is a famous teaser. Offhand I cannot tell you, but I will look it up when I get home.'

The sweet creature! She would look it up in her big Dante when she got home. What a woman!

'It occurred to me' she said 'apropos of I don't know what, that you might do worse than make up Dante's rare movements of compassion in Hell. That used to be' her past tenses were always sorrowful 'a favourite question.'

He assumed an expression of profundity.

'In that connexion' he said 'I recall one superb pun anyway:

"qui vive la pietà quando è ben morta . . ."'

She said nothing.

'Is it not a great phrase?' he gushed.

She said nothing.

'Now' he said like a fool 'I wonder how you could translate that?'

Still she said nothing. Then:

'Do you think' she murmured 'it is absolutely necessary to translate it?'

Sounds as of conflict were borne in from the hall. Then silence. A knuckle tamboured on the door, it flew open and lo it was Mlle Glain, the French instructress, clutching her cat, her eyes out on stalks, in a state of the greatest agitation.

'Oh' she gasped 'forgive me. I intrude, but what was in the bag?'

'The bag?' said the Ottolenghi.

Mlle Glain took a French step forward.

'The parcel' she buried her face in the cat 'the parcel in the hall.'

Belacqua spoke up composedly.

'Mine' he said, 'a fish.'

He did not know the French for lobster. Fish would do very well. Fish had been good enough for Jesus Christ, Son of God, Saviour. It was good enough for Mlle Glain.

'Oh' said Mlle Glain, inexpressibly relieved, 'I caught him in the nick of time.' She administered a tap to the cat. 'He would have tore it to flitters.'

Belacqua began to feel a little anxious.

'Did he actually get at it?' he said.

'No no' said Mlle Glain 'I caught him just in time. But I did not know' with a blue-stocking snigger 'what it might be, so I thought I had better come and ask.'

Base prying bitch.

The Ottolenghi was faintly amused.

'Puisqu'il n'y a pas de mal . . .' she said with great fatigue and elegance.

'Heureusement' it was clear at once that Mlle Glain was devout 'heureusement'.

Chastening the cat with little skelps she took herself off. The grey hairs of her maidenhead screamed at Belacqua. A devout, virginal blue-stocking, honing after a penny's worth of scandal.

'Where were we?' said Belacqua.

But Neapolitan patience has its limits.

'Where are we ever?' cried the Ottolenghi, 'where we were, as we were.'

Belacqua drew near to the house of his aunt. Let us call it Winter, that dusk may fall now and a moon rise. At the corner of the street a horse was down and a man sat on his head. I know, thought Belacqua, that that is considered the right thing to do. But why? A lamplighter flew by on his bike, tilting with his pole at the standards, jousting a little yellow light into the evening. A poorly dressed couple stood in the bay of a pretentious gateway, she sagging against the railings, her head lowered, he standing facing her. He stood up close to her, his hands dangled by his sides. Where we were, thought Belacqua, as we were. He walked on, gripping his parcel. Why not piety and pity both, even down below? Why not mercy and Godliness together? A little mercy in the stress of sacrifice, a little mercy to rejoice against judgment. He thought of Jonah and the gourd and the pity of a jealous God on Nineveh. And poor Mc-Cabe, he would get it in the neck at dawn. What was he doing now, how was he feeling? He would relish one more meal, one more night.

His aunt was in the garden, tending whatever flowers die at that time of year. She embraced him and together they went down into the bowels of the earth, into the kitchen in the basement. She took the parcel and undid it and abruptly the lobster was on the table, on the oilcloth, discovered.

'They assured me it was fresh' said Belacqua.

Suddenly he saw the creature move, this neuter creature. Definitely it changed its position. His hand flew to his mouth.

'Christ!' he said 'it's alive.'

His aunt looked at the lobster. It moved again. It made a faint nervous act of life on the oilcloth. They stood above it, looking down on it, exposed cruciform on the oilcloth. It shuddered again. Belacqua felt he would be sick.

'My God' he whined 'it's alive, what'll we do?'

The aunt simply had to laugh. She bustled off to the pantry to fetch her smart apron, leaving him goggling down at the lobster, and came back with it on and her sleeves rolled up, all business.

'Well' she said 'it is to be hoped so, indeed.'

'All this time' muttered Belacqua. Then, suddenly aware of her hideous equipment: 'What are you going to do?' he cried.

'Boil the beast' she said, 'what else?'

'But it's not dead' protested Belacqua 'you can't boil it like that.'

She looked at him in astonishment. Had he taken leave of his senses?

'Have sense' she said sharply, 'lobsters are always boiled alive. They must be.' She caught up the lobster and laid it on its back. It trembled. 'They feel nothing' she said.

In the depths of the sea it had crept into the cruel pot. For hours, in the midst of its enemies, it had breathed secretly. It had survived the French-woman's cat and his witless clutch. Now it was going alive into scalding water. It had to. Take into the air my quiet breath.

Belacqua looked at the old parchment of her face, grey in the dim kitchen.

'You make a fuss' she said angrily 'and upset me and then lash into it for your dinner.'

She lifted the lobster clear of the table. It had about thirty seconds to live.

Well, thought Belacqua, it's a quick death, God help us all.

It is not.